For B,

Without whom I could not be myself. Who doesn't judge me and look at me strange when I talk about the 'crazy' in my head. Who helps me with my stories when I'm stuck; sometimes making things even better.

Lydia is spending Christmas alone for the first time. At least her house is beautifully decorated.

"When he finally comes to, his bloodied and swollen eyes connect with mine. I'm sure a part of him is wondering, but the bigger and more deviant part of him doesn't care that I'm on top of him, or why his cock is inside of me."

My

Christmas

Story

By Rayne Havok

Warning

I'm told this should have an 'extreme' warning.

Because these things are always in my head and on my mind, I don't always consider them to be over-the-top. To some it may be run-of-the mill and to others it may be too much.

If you feel like you may have issues reading 'extreme' stories, please don't bother with this one, you may be offended.

ONE

The cuckoo clock on the wall tells me it's 11:15pm. Every time I look at it I'm reminded of one of our European trips, this one took us to Germany, where it is practically mandatory to leave with one.

We'd chosen well, I think, the clock had spoken to both of us, with its intricate design and beautiful craftsmanship. We'd known right away this was perfect for us. It's small, having to fit in a bag to take on the airplane back to the states, but somehow commands the space on the wall where it hangs.

A constant reminder of my love for him. We had gone for our one year wedding anniversary, it was a trip I could never forget. During that vacation, if I really thought about it, had been the moment I truly and fully fell in love with Henry. I had always loved him, this was simply the spot I could pinpoint it falling into place, knowing it would last forever. He had finally made his way into my heart and it grew to the point that only his love filled the space in there.

I sigh, the thoughts of him looking so happy and full of life and potential. I almost lose a tear from my eye but, I smile through it.

The tree is especially beautiful now, I'd put some finishing touches on it tonight. We'd put the tree up together right after Thanksgiving, one of our many traditions; always so excited for this time of year.

In fact, Christmas day is our wedding anniversary. Both of us knowing right away that it would be the only day that would encompass us and mean the most.

Our celebration together would have happened in about an hour from now, and here I sit, alone for the first time in all our years. The first time I've had to wait alone for the clock on the wall to sound midnight, making it officially our day and marking another year. This would have been twenty.

This time the tear does fall and then another. How am I supposed to do this without him? How am I supposed to fill this house with Christmas cheer without the person that had been my source of happiness for all these years?

I can't think about it anymore. The fact is, he isn't coming back; he won't be here for anymore anniversaries or Christmases. I will be doing it without him. I'm filled with a loneliness so deep it tears my chest apart and my throat seizes up.

I can wish and hope all I want, but, the facts are the facts and no amount of wishing or hoping can bring somebody back to me.

My head falls back onto the head rest behind me and my eyes close. I have to be strong right now. This is a new journey in my life; I am alone and without my partner. And, in less than an hour, I will ring in our anniversary alone. First of many. This will be the hardest, my loss still so new. It should begin to get easier after this, as each year passes; so they say.

The thought settles me. I will be ok– I have to be.

I walk over to the tree, his gift for me underneath. I have no idea what it is, even though I had been looking at credit card statements, trying to see. He must have used cash.

I hate surprises, contradicting my love for Christmas. But, it was never about the gifts for me, it was about all the love everyone feels during this time of the year.

The box is large, I lift it– heavy.

The modern gift for twenty years is platinum. I was expecting a piece of jewelry, even though I've never been the type for anything other than my wedding ring. I thought, like me, he would have gotten me a replacement band. I went to the best jeweler and picked the nicest band I thought would fit him well and engraved "you own me" into it.

I've always felt that way, he truly had owned me. My life consisted only of pleasing him, making sure to show and tell him every chance I got. Now, I'm out of time.

This box tells me he hadn't thought about it even though we had stuck to that tradition, starting out loosely; selecting only the ones we liked. We had made it a tradition once we'd begun to truly love finding just the right thing to fit under those guidelines. I had been hinting at what could be a great idea for months leading up to the holiday.

I wipe at my arm absentmindedly when a drop falls onto it.

I pull at the beautiful bow tied around the large box. Had never been one for wrapping so this had been prepared by the gift- services wrappers. I never minded. It was sweet that he knew I love beautiful wrapping but was unable to attain that level himself.

I myself, always took my time to gently and lovingly wrap his gifts. He would tear into them like a child though, always too excited for theatrics. I never thought it uncouth, just loved seeing his joy.

Another drop.

I get through the paper, shiny and thick; good quality. The box gives nothing away, it's simply a brown cardboard. I pull at the tape and it gives way; unfolding the flaps I see instantly what it is. A mother fucking blender. I'm absolutely shattered. That bastard. It was a slap in the face if I've ever seen one.

I bet that *bitch* got something. I bet whore woman fucked him until he forked over whatever the fuck she wanted, sucked his cock like some come guzzling vampire. I know what he was like.

Insatiable. Needing it often and everywhere. I was mistaken to think that I would be enough.

It took a lot to confront him with what I had found. The emails I should have seen long ago, the texts he'd not even hidden; I'd simply been stupid enough to trust him. Being so in love myself, I was unable to see what was in front of me; the longer evenings at work, the need for more and more time away from me.

I just thought it was his need to be successful in his career; never having kids pushed him to excel at work. I had sacrificed my time with him for him to have his purpose.

I wanted him to be happy, and he was, but it had been her more recently, *Ashley–* from the name on the emails. The sweet things he'd been saying to her in them, all the love and kind words he wrote her. I read all the happiness he had for her and all the times he had told her he'd wished he was with her and stuck here… with me.

It shattered me to read those things. How could I have been so fucking stupid? How had I been unable to sense it? I had lived with this man for twenty fucking years. How had I lost him; I'd catered to his every whim, sexually and otherwise.

He was a demanding man, he knew what he wanted and I wanted it for him. I wanted to be the one to give it to him, no matter what. I wanted to please him in every way. All his kinky and wild fantasies, I needed to be the source of fulfillment in those. I did everything for him.

Reading those emails told me he'd been getting them met by her as well. I know that had he told me he wanted another woman I would have done anything to find just the right girl and invite her to share our bed, for him. I think he knew that. So, I have to assume he had meant to leave me this whole time– since the moment this started with her. Possibly just waiting for the right moment to devastate me.

Another drop, this time I look at the source.

"Oh, Henry, I wish you'd continued to be a good man." I finger a part of him now; the source of the dripping. The piece of him I'd ripped from his torso; slick and wet, hung neatly, woven around the branches in true garland fashion. Who knew intestines would look so beautiful wrapped around a Pine. And there was plenty to decorate with, much longer out of the body than I realized.

Two

Earlier that night…

I wait patiently for Henry to make it home, allegedly at work– after what I've learned I can't even believe that any more.

I hear the front door close quietly, he calls out to me. "Lydia?"

"In here." I stay seated in my arm chair. I take a deep breath, trying to steady my beating heart.

He stops in the door way of our neatly decorated living room. "How was your day, love?"

Love? Was he fucking kidding me? "Fine, how was work?" I say sweetly.

"Oh, you know, same old shit, different day." He empties his pockets of wallet and change, coming toward me. I'm sure he expects his devoted wife to be more welcoming than I am.

"You ok?" he asks, knowing me too well to let my mood go unnoticed.

"Fine." I say shortly, which only leads him to inquire again.

"You don't look fine, something must be the matter." He comes to sit with me on my seat, I don't scoot to give him room, so he is left to half hover on the cushion.

He reaches out to me, touching my face softly with the back of his hand.

It infuriates me that my body responds to his touch like it always had. That gives me the final push to tell him what I've uncovered.

"I know about Ashley." I say unceremoniously.

His face pales. I see the pulse in his throat quicken. He doesn't try and deny it. I'm grateful for that. What he does say doesn't ease any of my pain though. "I was wondering when this might happen."

It's my turn for shock. My hands begin to shake and I can't hold back the anger I feel; the heat of my body radiating. "What the fuck have you done, Henry?"

"I was going to tell you after the holidays."

"Tell me what? Why don't you share it with me now?"

He moves to his own seat, the matching pair to my own. "I never meant to hurt you; I don't want this to be over."

I can see in his eyes he is telling me what he *thinks* I want to hear. My fingernails dig into my palm. Rage brews inside me.

"I don't know what you know." He seems to wait for me to fill him in, and when I don't, he continues. "I met her at work; she was a temp a few months ago. It means nothing...meant nothing." He corrects himself.

"So then, it's over? You can end it with her?" I'm only trying to get a read on him, I know from the email sent last night that they had plans for New Years– a get-away. And with that being the time we go on a trip ourselves, he was going to make the break with me between now and then.

"Of course, sweetie. She won't come between us, we have so much together."

The lies from his mouth flow so eloquently that I'm sure he's learned along the way how to manipulate me. And he thinks he is doing it now.

"Really Henry?" I go overboard on the hopefulness in my voice and he doesn't notice; he thinks he's maintaining the upper hand.

I slink from my chair, landing on my knees I crawl toward him. I see the arousal hit him. After all these years he knows what is coming, his hands itch to move for his zipper, but he knows he shouldn't assume that's what might be happening right now.

I crawl my hands up his legs and unzip him. His cock is already hard, throbbing as I take it in my hand. I hold his eyes with mine as I bring my mouth to the wet tip; working him the way I know drives him crazy. Deep and hard. I relax my throat and let it pass my tonsils.

He groans loudly, gripping the knot of hair on my head, he moves my head and his hips in unison, fucking hard against my mouth. I can feel him close to his finish and pull away from him. The question is in his eyes, but he doesn't ask it.

I stand and pull him up with me. I undress him quickly and then myself. He tries to touch me but I back away, playing coy. I widen my legs and touch my pussy, sliding my fingers through the slit; I rub my clit. His breathing quickens and his hand moves to his cock, pumping quickly.

My heart is pounding so hard as I walk to him and reach into his hair, the beautifully lush head of hair I'd run my fingers through countless times while he lays in bed waiting for sleep to catch up to him. I wrap my fingers around it and drag him roughly to his knees. I push his face into my pussy and his tongue instantly goes to work. I let him taste me even though I'm furious. I'm hardly ever demanding, so this is a treat for him. He loves the occasions I take control and force him to do these things– to an extent. He would never relinquish it completely.

I pull his head back and lean over to kiss him, his mouth taste like me. This time when I bring his head forward it's my knee it hits. Hard. Like the self-defense classes have taught me. I bet he regrets having talked me into going to them now as his nose explodes. The crack is loud in the quiet room.

I turn my wrist and force his face upward to me, the shocked look in his eyes sends me over the edge and I laugh, "You stupid fuck!" I smash his face again with the heel of my palm, shoving his nose upward. His body becomes slack as his lights go out, landing hard against the wood floor.

I'd always been so demure, so submissive to him. He must have taken that to mean weak this whole time. My small frame only adding to it, I suppose. The feeling that is in me now must be all of that pent up, because I feel euphoric. I never knew this lived in me.

I take advantage of this feeling and the fact that he is out cold and get a sheet from the linen closet. I roll him onto it and as I'm dragging him he comes to.

Quickly remembering his predicament, he moves fast, but not faster than me. I'm on him before he can roll to his knees and make his escape.

Situating his arms at his hips, I kneel on his hands and straddle his lap. He starts to say something but my fist landing against his jaw stops him. I hit him over and over. I've never punched anyone my whole life, but something deep inside me knows just how to deliver them, avoiding his teeth so to not bloody my knuckles on them.

I feel his jaw loosen, teeth giving way, as my strikes become more furious and forceful; sweat pouring from my hair, into my eyes, as the effort to keep the pace with my hatred pushes my body to the limits. The adrenaline taking over, which is why I don't see right away that he is out again.

I stop, breathless. His mouth slack and empty looking from the loss of teeth. I pull his lips back to survey the damage, removing the lost teeth as far back as his throat. I collect eight whole and two fragments. I place them in the candy dish we had set out for decoration on the coffee table. They give it a more appropriate feel for this Christmas.

I drag his limp body with the overhang of the sheet to the vintage radiator that sits under the window. I go in search of a few items to restrain him.

I unload an armful of items next to him. Zip tying his arms above his head to the radiator and tie a thick rope around his ankles, and the other end tightly to the exposed support beam in the middle of the room to keep his legs in place.

When he finally comes to, his bloodied and swollen eyes connect with mine. I'm sure a part of him is wondering, but the bigger and more deviant part of him doesn't care why I'm on top of him, or why his cock is inside of me.

He seems to have forgotten all about me lashing out on his face and that he is restrained. He pushes that aside somehow, bucking his hips up repeatedly to meet my pace. I bounce on him, the way he likes, the way that makes my tits bounce like a porn star; the way that makes him come the hardest.

"I bet she doesn't know how to fuck you like I can, how to make you feel so fucking good."

I slow my pace and squeeze my pussy tightly around him. He moans, completely lost in this.

"I bet she doesn't feel this good wrapped around your big cock." I rub myself, sitting hard on his thighs; shoving every inch inside of me. My fingers working fast.

He tries to watch, but is unable to get the angle to see so he looks at my face instead, his eyes holding mine as he watches me enjoy myself.

My breath comes faster as I climb closer to my finish. I let out a shaky moan as I finally come. Leaning over his heaving chest, I kiss his mouth, sucking his bottom lip; tasting the blood that has settled and dried there.

Pulling myself off his still overly- swollen cock, I kiss down his chest until I reach it with my lips. It's glistening with my come and I taste myself on him as I suck his dick into my mouth. It fills my throat as I swallow it down, fucking him with only my mouth until I taste the hint of come settle on my taste buds. I pull up on it, licking around the head, salivating at the taste of us together.

"Does she make you feel this good?"

"No. Never." He breathes. And I believe him. I know what makes this man; I know everything that makes him tick. He may have wanted something different, but if I wanted him to, I know I could have him back. I know, if I could forgive him, we could be so good together, still. But I can't. And won't.

I bite down teasingly on the head of his cock, purple from being without release. He cries out excitedly. I lick him and push it down my throat again, sucking hard all the way up the length– slowly, over and over; all the way up and then down again, milking him. Quickening the rhythm until I feel the tell- tale stiffening before the finish.

Just as I taste his semen on my tongue I drag the box cutter across the base of his cock, above his empting balls. He doesn't feel it at first, too caught up in the release and somehow it makes it more erotic for me, the come exploding in my mouth and the blood mingling as I work him through his finish.

I know the second he feels the cut, my saliva bringing it alive, and still one more pulse of come evacuates.

I replace my mouth with my hand and the look in his eyes, as I lick my lips to collect the fluid mixture around my mouth, tells me he is well aware of my intentions now. I show him, this time, the source of his pain, the box cutter I had stashed next to us for this purpose. Pulling up on his cock, making it taught, I dig the blade into his flesh and circle around until it comes off in my hand, finishing the job.

I hold his cock up to his face, pale from shock. His face contorts as I lick the head, the sound that comes from him is one of fear. Pure terror. Not even the loss of his cock is as horrible as seeing me blow it now, after it's been removed.

He sees the side of me that I've been able to keep hidden, the side he's been keeping at bay with his love. Now that that is gone, I let myself out of the cage.

My lips make a popping sound as I pull his cock from my mouth. "And now it's too late for poor *Ashley* to try harder to please you."

His bleeding gets out of hand, but I don't try and stop it. "Don't worry, it doesn't seem like you're going to have to live too much longer without it."

"What the fuck? You crazy bitch!" he shouts.

"Oh, honey, I wouldn't yell at the woman who literarily holds your cock in her hand. Doesn't seem smart." I boop him on the nose with it.

He looks shocked that this could be happening to him, it fuels a rage inside of me. I want to rip him apart, this man who had promised me a forever with him has ended it for some pussy, he himself, has said is not up to par with mine. This man who promised 'till death do us part'. I thought it would have been a more natural type of death, but he's brought this on himself and now it's one of my doing.

I watch his eyes fall heavy and become slow to open. "Do you have anything you want to say before we begin?" I ask.

"Before we *begin*? You're holding my dick in your hand! How have we *not* begun? That should be the end."

"Oh, honey, I don't think I could live without you having a cock. You know how much I love it."

He loses it then. "Are you going to *kill* me?"

"You killed yourself when you started this whole thing with her, when you stuck this," I hold his cock up again, "inside of her; you killed yourself." then toss it aside.

"So, nothing to say, then?" I slide the razor across his thigh. Blood dots and the gathers together then falls down either side of his leg, pooling on the sheet.

"Bitch." He says through gritted teeth. "You can't do this to me, you fucking cunt." His voice betrays him and cracks in fear.

"I think I am doing this. And your insults are lacking."

I push the triangle edge of the blade into his skin as deep as it will go and drag it a couple of inches, the blood is pouring out of this one. I climb up his body and slash repeatedly at his arms, I move quickly, cutting his flesh. Exes mark from wrists to armpits.

He opens the flood gate of his lungs and cries sobs of fear and hatred for me.

I slap his face, trying to bring him back. "Shut the fuck up, Henry."

He does no such thing, if anything; he gets louder and more frantic.

"Shut. The. Fuck. Up. Henry." I shout over him.

When he still will not heed my words, I reach down to his feet and grab his cock, shoving it deep into his wide open mouth, mid scream, closing my hand over it to keep it inside.

When attached, it was close to eight inches, it probably lost an inch in the removal process, and limp now– giving room for manipulation; he shares none of my throat- opening- dick- sucking skills himself. He is choking and the screams have become frantic heaves. His eyes are watering now, no longer from fear, they're flowing freely from gagging.

"Do you want to die like this, Henry? With your cock vying for a spot in your throat, or do you want to die with dignity? It's up to you."

I sit back onto my heels and wait for him to make his choice. He calms himself, as much as a man with his own cock shoved down his throat can, so, I take my hand from his mouth. The appendage folds out, sliding down his cheek and flops to the floor.

His chest heaves, trying to replenish the air. He regains some composure quickly.

"Shall we continue now?" I drag the razor from his adam's apple to the vee- juncture of my thighs, at his belly button. Blood fills the line and I slide my finger along the incision, not deep enough to do anything other than superficial damage. But, he doesn't seem to know that, the pain is overwhelming.

I run my hands through the blood on his arms, painting him in it, then smear it across my breasts, squeezing my always- hard nipples. I wasn't prepared for this to be so erotic. My pussy tingles from the sight of him restrained and red, slices marring his always-perfect looking skin. "Fuck, Henry, you look so sexy right now. I'm going to use this image for years to come."

I cut at him again, over his chest, the slashing is quick and deep; gaping in many spots. His screams are back, hitting me right between my legs, but, this time I revel in them. I grind myself against his belly, slick with blood, I slide freely; the pressure building quickly. "If I'd have known this would be so hot I'd have left your cock attached until the end." I rock harder against him, pushing my fingers against my clit. My breath coming almost frantic as I reach for my finish.

Coming down from my orgasm, I realize that his screams have stopped and that I had been leveraging myself on his throat; like he often loved me to do. I check his pulse, it's still there; shallow, but there.

I look down at our bodies, mine– tingling in the orgasmic aftermath. Red and slick with wetness;

slathered in the blood of the man I'd been more in love with than myself and now, I'm getting off on his bloodied body. I look beautiful, more alive than I ever have. His– barely holding on.

I hit his face to rouse him, smacking lightly at first, but when nothing happens and I start hitting him harder. Something takes over, I stop trying to wake him and the hate overwhelms me.

This face that looked at me in the morning and made love to me. This face that kissed me 'goodnight' every night and fucked me until I was exhausted enough for sleep. The face that I had memorized and loved, who loved me back so deeply there were never any secrets. Until there was one. *Her.* The reason I will be alone now, the reason for hatred when I look into his beautiful face, the reason I can't stop my arms from lashing out at him now. She did this– and he let her.

His face is split and actively bleeding, I realize quickly that I've got the blade in my hand and that I've been gouging his cheek and throat; the arterial spray alerting me, quite vividly, that this will be the end. Blood is pulsing quickly out of his body like a geyser, spraying me and the walls. I watch as it dies down to a stream, coming quickly still.

I don't miss him as he slips away, I don't have any remorse. He had brought this upon himself, his death is on *his* hands.

I do miss the man I thought he was, though; the idea of our forever. I hold on to the years that were good, the idea that he was mine for that time. He still is, in fact, this part of him will always be mine.

I climb off his body and go in search for what I need to finish the job, coming back with an arm full of tools. I kneel next to him, leaning over his chest to make the first cut– the Y incision performed in an autopsy I've seen countless times depicted on the crime shows we loved to watch.

He hasn't been refrigerated which is why, I assume, there is blood seeping from the wound I create at his shoulder blade. Either that or TV just gives the illusion it's less messy. The razor slices through easily, the thin layer of fat on top of his muscle he carried around his midsection needs another inch or so to get deep enough to see his insides.

It surprises me that there are varying shades of pink and flesh toned pieces, slimy and wet looking. I cut along the sinew that hold his flesh to his ribs, finally pulling it back; enabling me to expose everything.

I remove the already tumbling intestines and set them aside, clamping before cutting, knowing the smell of what's inside would be much worse than what I've already encountered. It leaves him almost hollow looking– they really take up a lot of space in there.

Reaching for the center of his rib cage, I take the knife I use in the kitchen for deboning. It takes a few sawing motions before I'm able to make progress, but, as soon as it's in there I'm able to slice through the bone. I take a triangle piece from it and set it aside, exposing what lies beneath.

His heart; I reach for it right away, cutting the pulmonary veins, thick as my finger and set it aside. Next the lungs liver and spleen, cutting the connective tissue that hold each organ in place.

Hollowed and empty, I feel a bit of vindication, knowing I've made him as empty as he's made me.

I cut at the skin around his neck and pull it over his face, cutting where I need to along the way to remove the skin and hair from his head. Essentially scalping him from front to back. His skull looks nothing like I thought it would. Nothing like him.

I send the cleaver through the neck bone a few times until it detaches. I hold up his skinned face to mine and look into his empty dead eyes.

Grabbling a stake- like piece of wood I'd found in the backyard– left over kindling for the fire pit. I find the softer part at the base of his neck and push them together hard enough to pierce. I hold it up by the shaft and walk him over to the tree, tying a long piece of twine around it and the stem of the tree a few inches from the top where it is thick enough to hold the weight. I replace the star at the top with his head, stepping back, I admire it. It's leaning a little, but, I don't mind.

I unwind his intestines and rope them around the front of the tree, back and forth until they're gone– a garland of intestines. Beautiful. I put his heart in my stocking, giving it as a gift to myself. I quickly remove his balls and replace the mistletoe with them, I chuckle at the thought of kissing under them, something he'd always loved for me to do. That soft tissue of his taint always his favorite to have teased.

More of his teeth into the candy dish, and the other organs become part of the decorations.

I sit back into my arm chair, and fully naked, drenched in the spray of blood, covering me in the most erotic way, I catch sight of his amputated cock and I have nothing more to use it for but a tool to get off right now.

It's heavy in my hand and I crave the feel of it inside of me, so that is where I put it, hitting the spot I need it to, and though I can't fuck it– its flaccid, I push my pussy against the chair and hold it inside of me as I work my clit. Rocking my hips against the edge of the chair, wildly bucking as I fuck myself. My pussy convulses with the oncoming orgasm and, lost in the depraved nature of what I'm doing I come a second time, launching his cock a full foot in front of me, flopping to the floor.

Coming down from my orgasms doesn't stop me from laughing at what happened.

THREE

The cuckoo clock chimes twelve times, alerting me of our day– our Christmas anniversary that will be my first alone.

Kicking the blender box with my foot as I take my feet, I stand and admire the beautiful scene; how my husband has made the room feel even more like a home.

I climb up the stairs, into our– now my– bed. Still covered in his blood, not bothering to shower, knowing as soon as I wake I'll have an awful mess to clean. I fall asleep quickly.

EPILOGUE

One year later…

I take the next box down from the top of the closet– the tree topper from last year. I saved it, after cleaning his skull, wrapping it and putting it away. I wanted him to spend the future Christmases with me as a reminder of us. "Hey, honey." I say to it after unfolding the flaps of cardboard.

I set it with the other boxes.

I test the lights, like I do before stringing them. I realize there are a few strands that will need replacing, not making it for this season. I put that on the list of things to get at the store.

Having finished going through the boxes, I grab my purse and the list off the table and I head out.

My cart is full of all things Christmas and I'm reaching high upon a shelf for the last few boxes of the multicolored lights I love, when I'm interrupted by a man.

"Would you like help?" he asks.

"Thank you." I step back to let him have room.

"I just love Christmas; it's my favorite." His eyes meet mine and ignites a fire inside me.

The smile that crosses my face is electric– like our connection. "Mine, too." I breathe.

I don't know if we'd make it twenty years– or a week for that matter. But, I look at him and know just the spot I'll put him when it ends.

The End

Thank you for taking the time to read.

Let me know what you thought by leaving a quick review.

Printed in Great Britain
by Amazon